BALTIMORE
KILLER HILL

SUNNI RINGGOLD

First Edition

NEWMAN SPRINGS PUBLISHING
320 Broad Street
Red Bank, NJ 07701

First originally published by Newman Springs Publishing 2022

ISBN 978-1-68498-444-2 (Paperback)
ISBN 978-1-68498-446-6 (Digital)

Printed in the United States of America

To Niles Ringgold

PROLOGUE

Clouds of smoke blanketed the air as one rolled over in the den. She pushed and shook him while choking on that little glass rose (small glass smoking tube). Really didn't want to offend him because crack was all over the den. Her addiction was way more important than waking up this dude.

"Zee-Zee," she said, still inhaling crack, coughing, trying to move away.

"Zee, it's mad dough out there."

"Say no more." Yo hopped right up rubbing the cold out of his eyes.

"What time is it?" he asked.

Choking, she replied, "It's nine thirty." Gasping, she took another hit.

"That bet not be none of my shit either! An' why the fuck is you smoking all this coke around me while I'm sleep! Looks like a sauna in this bitch! Gotta hold my breath in here before I catch contact. Where is my stuff at? I'm up out this shack. Hold up. Where the fuck my pills at?"

"You know you keep your shit in the bando," Pipe Head said.

"Nah, they the dopes. I had some readdies (crack cocaine) on me! An' who the fuck is that in the kitchen 'cause he about to get it! An' you too 'cause you've been smoking all night!" Zee said.

"Boy! I am not gonna steal shit from you; you always have big 'do right by me.' All I gotta do is ask, and you will give it to me," Pipe Head said.

Zee said, "Right! So why the hell I can't find my shit! An' who else was in here because somebody 'bout to get it then"—*he quickly paused*—"my bad. Here it goes! I forgot I hid it in the cushion after I hit you and Nita last night. No brush to the mouth, straight fireman shit. Soon, as a bother comes out the front door, they are on it! They all in a nigga face 'bout fifty fiends on the chase! One never liked to jump straight out there. So he gives a look around, and nobody's around. Anyway, stick to the routine…Honey Bun, Pepsi, and a loose one single cigarette for breakfast. Plus, he needs to get the info on what's happened out here. Yeah!" A smile of relief came to Zee's face. His day 1 comrade, G-dawg, was on the corner with some mophead.

"Wit it do, Pimp?" Zee asked.

"Shit," G-dawg replied. "Chillin 'bout to hit the bar with little mama."

"How it look out this bitch?" Zee asked.

"You see wit it do! Nothing out here but action! So you know what that mean," G-dawg replied.

"Hot dough! Police everywhere, nobody out!" Zee said.

They began to laugh…

"No, Ass! They out this whore deep! An' I ain't fucking with you, Zee!" G-dawg said.

"Lemme get a cigarette—never mind, I'ma grab one from the store. I need a soda anyway. My mouth is dry," Zee said.

As he began to walk in the store, Zee ran back out to tell G-dawg…

"Yo, don't roll out on me!" Zee said.

CHAPTER 1

Buss 'Em Up! (Eluding Police)

"FUCK, YOU BEEN at, Yo? Where your little mophead go?" Zee asked.

"She was on some other shit. I don't know where she went," G-dawg said.

"Man, they out this joint like zombies walking on roaches. Wit it do though, Dawg. You trying to hit this action with me?" Zee asked.

"You must be gonna hit them 'cause it's fire out this bitch," G-dawg said.

"Love, you know I fuck with that 'Hot Dough,'" said Zee.

G-dawg replied, "All right, you go ahead an' fuck with it then."

"Yo, you got me or not?" Zee asked.

"You stay on your jerk shit. Fuck it, let's get it," G-dawg said.

"Look right, send them all to Mr. Spencer's old yard," Zee said.

"For what?" G-dawg asked.

"I'm not that dumb. I'm not fucking with that block; they on it! We're gonna send them to the other side. I'ma hit 'em over there. Go ahead and round them up and watch the split for me while I grab them things real quick," Zee said.

"Bet," G-dawg said.

Now as G-dawg began to round them up, the dickheads were in covert somewhere. The thing was, they were not on G-dawg and Zee. They followed the sheep to the slaughter. Meanwhile, Zee was in the bando fumbling through trash, clothes, and old furniture.

This was Jim's old house, which was directly across Jefferson Street from Mr. Spencer's.

Creeping out of the front door of the bando (abandoned house) and skipping across Jefferson Street to Mr. Spencer's, Zee ran through Spencer's old house to the backyard where G-dawg had all the fiends at.

Now back here in this alley on the other side, niggas call it "Snake Alley" because of its three ways in from Port and three ways in from Montford with a split running through the middle of the three alleys.

Anyway, as soon as Zee came through the backdoor, action (sale, drug addict) was everywhere. G-dawg had about fifty fiends all roundup in the yard. I mean, it looked like they were giving out Ts (testers, free drugs). *Bam!* Zee got to it, giving it up! Then Zee saw a fiend walk past the split down in the middle alley.

A white boy with a red hoodie, at least one thought he was a fiend until Zee waved him on.

"Come on, Yo! Fuck you over there for?"

Then he pulled out that fucking radio!

Zee's face dropped. "Oh shit…"

Why the fuck didn't G-dawg call out nothing? Zee wondered in his mind. But fuck all that, only time to react. So Zee got out of there! Pushing and knocking junkies over and all! He hit the alley running toward the block. In Zee's mind, he questioned himself on why he didn't just run back through the house. So G-dawg was at the bottom of the alley looking as dumbfounded as Zee while Zee was running toward him.

Now picture G-dawg's face: he realized that nigga ain't know what was going on. Anyway, Zee just remembered jumping on a pile of snow then into the street. And G-dawg was looking at Zee as if they were in a motion movie. If you think about it, there are six ways in Snake Alley: three from each side. Guess they ran down on him and G-dawg from the Montford side. They must've followed the flock coming in or going out. Nevertheless, Zee's feet hit Port Street; before he could get to Jefferson, here they come. Little black Chevy

Cavalier, Yo with the red hood was on Zee's heels! Zee left his ass behind in the alley.

This shit was really thrilling. All you hear were car tires screeching coming from around Montford. Zee hopped Jefferson street like a gazelle; once Zee hit the block, he prayed for a plot. Then it came to Zee: his run plan. Taking y'all through this real quick 'cause that's how quick a nigga bust; they ass up! Zee hit the block in stride. Now Brenda's house was the corner house with no fence at the yard. There was a brick wall that separated Brenda's from Loco's yard, which was the second house with Mandie's yard next, then Jim's old house where you had to go through the window from off the back porch.

Let's get it! In motion, he hit Brenda's yard sharp. Zee saw the split by the back steps in Brenda's yard into Loco's. Zee slid through the little split, hopped across Loco's yard, and over the wall into Mandie's yard. Now that Zee was in Mandie's yard, which was the third house, he ran up her backdoor steps, then jumped over to Jim's porch and went right through the window.

Going through the window, Zee gave a glance back and the look on the police's face was like, "Damn, this fucker is good!" Now this was when things became interesting because they thought they got Zee because they saw him went into the house. So you know they were out front, but Zee's protocol was to hit the roof and Zee get straight to it when he comes through the window!

Now there was a skylight in the backroom that Zee had left open on another geek run. This time it was *for real*, and he gave it up (hustling, expeditiously) to the backroom. He had to get a chair or something to get up there, and he didn't really remember what it was. But the drop ceiling, skylight, whatever you call it, it was in the backroom. So as soon as Zee set his ass on the roof, this bitch looked right in his face! "Assholes on the roof now," he called into his radio. Zee ran to the middle of the roof in a crouched position. *Been through this before*, Zee thought to himself. He ran up to the corner store. As he was running across the roof, he started dropping pills down peoples' chimneys. Now Zee knew they were about to call in for the bird (helicopter).

So whatever Zee was gonna do, he had better do it quickly because they were on their shit. The corner store has a little ledge, about a foot and a half wide. Zee gave a glimpse to see if any of those dickheads were there. *Fuck it*! Zee thought to himself, Zee hang-jumps to the little ledge. He was rearing back off the ledge; adrenaline was pumping, so he continued jumping.

Zee landed on one hand and one knee; some say he looked like "Spider Zee." He walked across the street taking off his peak coat and hid it under a car.

Zee began walking southbound toward Route 40. Now he had to walk past the alley on the other side of the street where the police were down at the other end. When Zee got to the alley, you wouldn't believe this shit so hilarious; when Zee hopped across the alley and glance down at it, this motherfucker was still looking up at the roof with the "dick-look." Zee got in the wind! He was walking down the street and noticed his home girl's door open—the house across the street though. Zee pondered a minute, *Hell with it*! *I'm on it*, Zee muttered to himself. Full blasting straight through her front door, breathing hard, hands and knees bleeding looking like a nigga just committed murder. To make things even more weird, this bitch landlord in the house eyeballed the shit out of Zee. Yo was cool though; he just looked at Zee all crazy and shit.

Bye quickly said, "Boy, go upstairs; take a bath or something."

Trying to get himself together, wondering if anyone saw him run in the house, Zee hauled his ass upstairs to the back window.

Now all you hear is the bird (helicopter) and police racing everywhere. At the window, watching his creation, with his bitch and a cunning smirk on his face, these dickheads were still in the alley by Jim's house. They were trying to figure out Zee's location while he was in covert on their dumb ass now. So it took them a minute to notice that he was gone.

Anyway, somehow, they walked to the corner and found Zee's coat, which was under the car. He tried to get Bye to grab it before they found it. For some reason, he knew that they were going to find it. His keys were in his pocket right along with some dough. He was kind of upset about that for a minute until he remembered he had a spare car key. Acting like he was mad at her for not going to get his coat because now it's time to smash(have sex).

Zee always wonders why women are attracted to the thrill of things. Start feeling on Bye's ass, now Bye body was that math with the soup cooling lips and all. Even though niggas always called Bye Tooth because her grill (mouth) was furred (mess up), they stayed packing (joking) on her. That body of hers made up for all of that space. Zee was all over her whispering sweet nothing in her ear. Slick legging (cunning in touching or like it's accidental) his love muscle from her ass to hips while he has her wrapped up with his arms. Bye felt him aroused; she pushed him away.

"Let's get high," she said.

He replied, "Say no more."

He told her to go out to G-dawg and get that loud (marijuana).

"Hope you didn't think I was going back out there," he said. "The day over with for me. I'm done, bout to jump in the tub, and grab something to drink." In his mind, he thought she's gonna need it because he planned on slaying her ass. Wow! You wouldn't believe that when Bye came back, Zee was in the deep sleep. Zee had fallen straight to sleep. Bye tried to wake him up, but his bones were in excruciating pain. He really couldn't move; everything just went stiff on him.

Grabbing Zee's arm and helping him to sit up, she asked, "You good?"

Zee gave a little groot. "Give me a sec. Where the grass at?" he asked.

His legs were numb, and Zee's arms were done. He was hoping the grass and drink would get him over the hump. Nipping it in the bud, he just laid back and smoked and didn't drink anything at all. He was pondering in his mind, high as a no bail, the lesson to be learned from his situation. Wondering how the hell he jumped off that roof like that, he was blaming it on the adrenaline running through his body.

Now feeling the finished product of the chase, he whispered to himself, "No pain, no buss 'em up."

CHAPTER 2

Silver Stirrups

All right, one night, Snot and Zee were standing on the corner of Port and Jefferson Street. Just then, out of the blue, they walked through Cookie and Cream. It was a playful way how their names came about. I couldn't remember how. This is one night one will never forget. Cream had these silver leggings on! She was so phat in them it didn't make the situation any better by her being so small. See, Cream was short, light-skinned, little bit of freckles on her face, and a next to nothing waist. Cookie was cool too, but Cream was a prize to be won. Guess what? She was the winner. Not just because she had the house down the street, although that was a plus. Cream was down to earth; her personality was benevolent. They had just moved around the way. Now they were coming from a little hole in the wall club around the corner. Once again, a sight to behold Cream with them silver leggings on. From then on, all comrades knew was that it was Cookie and Cream's house.

Would like to mention that Cream was a cradle robber. Even though one pursued her, she still knew a nigga was too young, eighteen or so, while she was about thirty-two at the time. A sweet old thang she was. For a young nigga to have a cougar on the team made things even more interesting. Cream became Zee's old lady. Her sister Cookie jumped around with a few of the dawgs. Nevertheless, Zee and Loco were banging the den out (chillin'). No matter the brand,

Zee always had the upper hand—the one who ran and made all the plans.

It was over for Cream once a young nigga laid that Mandingo on her ass. Yo looking at her phat ass, such a nice little red thang. "'Bout to trash that red ass," Zee said to himself. Because when push came to shove, Cream was really that! This was how you knew, how gone Cream was over the wood: thinking about the times Zee's feet had a vicious odor, she didn't mind and could care less. All she cared about was that muscle. Putting the boots under the bed trying to hide the smell. The freckles on her face always had a thing with Zee. Plus, Cream's voice was so attractive to him. It almost was like Fran from the sitcom *The Nanny* but not as loud and irky.

Zee ran up to her and grabbed that ass, then whispered in her ear, "Let's go upstairs." Cream looked back at him with this seductive face, shocking more than anything. Knowing Zee is always playing games with the pole. He kept her on the chase and for good reason. Cream didn't waste a minute running that ass up the steps, straight lusting off that ass as it bounced up the steps. Zee locked the door behind them. Cream flopped down on the bed; it was like they were synchronized or reading each other's minds. She damn near pulled his pants down with her mind. Zee was up on her whipping his sword out while she was tugging at his legs trying to snatch his pants off. He tried to put all ten inch in her mouth, grabbing on her head. She yanked away choking and gasping for air.

"Damn, boy! Fuck you, trying kill me?" Zee laughed as she continued to slide her tongue down the side of his mountain with tears in her eyes. She came from under the bottom holding the head of his muscle with her thumb. Nibbling lightly and kissing all the way to the top. She stopped and gave the head a quick pop in and out of her mouth. It was repeatedly done making a pop sound. Cream paused for a moment; she looked at it like it's a monster. Yet she is the one about to devour it. Open wide two only swallow half, try again a quarter inch more takes her wind. Third times a charm, fucking with that monster, her throat was about to be harmed—gagging with spit everywhere. She had to respect the mountain before it killed her.

Halfway down again and again with a moaning sound while she's twirling her head around, Zee can't take much more. He grabbed her and turned her around with her ass all in the air. Ripping her stirrups off from her hips, snatching her panties off, pussy jumped straight out at Zee. He grabbed her ass with both hands to spread it apart. He wasted no time sliding up in that twat. She was already soaking wet, dripping everywhere. Zee got to banging that twat from the back while opening up her ass as wide as he could.

One thing about Cream, she was infatuated with Zee muscle. She would take all she could whenever she could, throwing that ass back and all, moving side to side on the mountain. So friskie all over the muscle turned Zee on even more. He began to hit it on the angle with one leg up on the bed. Bring the wood down on her from a different position, switched legs and punish the other side. He was into it now, spitting all in her ass jamming his two fingers in her butt as he continued to fuck. Cream was about to explode; before then, she must take control. So she ran from the monster as Zee was still trying to grab hold of her hips. She slid to the side on the bed on her knees, took hold of his arms and laid him down on the bed.

See, Cream just had to be in control of her orgasm. She slithered on top of Zee as if she was a snake—legs, ass, and pussy all in one motion, sliding her hands across his chest while moving real slow on the muscle. She began to raise up, light stroking Zee's stomach with her nails. She came down on the mountain again, slowly twirling to kiss his chest and bite his nipples while she jiggles her hips with her hands. She grabbed the sides of Zee's ribs and twirled that twat to the top. Shaking her head while grinding and winding all over the sword. Zee had her by the waist admiring her stomach as he caressed her breast. He raised up to suck on them; they were just a handful to begin.

Now Zee was every bit of six feet two inches when Cream was only about five feet four inches, maybe five feet six inches. He just had to jump up off the bed and slam all muscle in her in the air. Her hands wrap around the back of his neck. He had one arm around her lower back, pounding while palming the left side of that ass. Zee banging away, she was hopping like it's the end of days. Then Cream began to slow down, wrapping her legs around him. Slowly grinding because she's all into it, shaking and moaning.

"What the fuck is these tears in her eyes" Zee said to himself. So he quickly turned her around and flopped down on the bed. The look on Cream's face was like the monster just bust her head open. Zee continued to bang, throwing her legs in the air, and then he exploded. Zee dropped next to her in the bed. Cream laid there for a second with a smile on her face of pure euphoria.

Just when you thought it was over, she grabbed his semi-hard love muscle and put it in her mouth and vacuumed the rest of Zee energy from his soul. Zee's eyes began to roll back. Cream looked up at him and gave a grin. Wow! Nigga's had a ball up in that den. Card games running through that joint and all types of parties. Till this day, Cream will always be a part of the Hill.

CHAPTER 3

Bubbles to Blaze

Making his way down the steps another early morning, Zee just finished smashing Cream (having sex) through the night. Loco was downstairs on the sofa. Zee was looking back at Cream on the steps with a cunning grin. She had an idea of what's about to go down yet not exactly what's going on in this dude's mind. She just knew he's one up to no good, aware of the games they play in the hood.

Sliding past Loco on the creep tip into the kitchen. Smiling on his silly shit, *Gotta get him* was running through his mind as he grabbed some dishwashing liquid while Loco was in the dining room with mouth wide open. Here we go, and Zee was on his dumb shit early in the morning. Loco was really still asleep while Zee squeezed at least half of the bottle down his throat. Before you know it, Loco popped up spitting and wiping his tongue. Cream and Zee were laughing hard. Zee was rolling all over the couch. This nigga was actually blowing bubbles. Loco was furious too, shaking his head at the zink washing his tongue off.

"Got 'em," Zee said to himself.

Loco was trying to talk shit, but Zee told him, "Wash that shit out your mouth." Loco sent all types of threats, and they just wired (lot of energy) laughing.

"I got y'all. Watch; mark my word. I'ma get you," Loco said.

Swinging at Zee with his other hand trying to land blows, Zee moved Cream in front of him packing (joking someone) all types of bubble jokes.

"That's fucked up!" Loco was yelling as he continued to wash the soap out his mouth. "Yo, this was supposed to be a safe haven for us," Loco said.

"It is safe, love; little bubbles ain't gonna hurt nobody," Zee said.

"You know what the fuck I mean!" Loco said.

Now Loco was Zee's ace, and eventually, they became like twins. How the hell does that happen don't start one lying. They didn't look anything alike, and Loco was about a buck ten (110) soaking wet. See dawg just went Loco because everybody used to bully him back in school. Also, the fact that he was on his local DJ phase didn't help. Plus, Loco was a nerd. Guess that's why he was so nice on the hustle tip. Loco really played with that math.

"Man, shut the fuck up, nigga; when you come up in her anyway?" Zee asked.

"Don't worry about it; you will know next time," Loco replied.

"Chess, my nigga, not checkers never catch me down bad. The *G* be chillin' up in the castle with the queen, door locked, and the hammer (gun pin) cocked. While you down this bitch dumbing, eyes wired shut, mouth wide open. Should have woken up when I slid past your silly ass the first time. Fuck all that; try and roll up the way or what? Zee asked.

"Fuck you, whore. I'm tryna go back to sleep," Loco replied.

Zee laughed when a bang at the door changed the mood. So you know the first thing a nigga was thinking was John-John (police).

"Who the fuck bangging at my damn door like that!" Cream yelled out.

Never was one so relieved to hear G-dawg's voice.

"It'z G-dawg. Is Zee in there?"

Thinking to himself, Zee was wondering what the hell G-dawg's drunk ass want, and why the fuck was he knocking like that.

Cream opened the door ready to give it to G's drunk ass.

"Why the fuck you knocking at my door like that! We all paranoid thinking you the law." Cream said.

"Where Zee at? Nardo house on fire!" G-dawg said.

Zee yelled. "What!" Pushing past Cream at the front of the door. "Wit it do, G?"

"Man, I don't know what happen up that bitch, that nigga up there crying, and some more shit," G-dawg said.

Zee jumped out the door heading up the way to the block with G-dawg on his hills.

CHAPTER 4

Little Body Bags

Now Nardo's house was in the block, well, Mrs. Bernice and Mr. Barren house. We called them the Barren's, and they were deep (a lot of) to. It was said they all had lead poison; as a matter of fact, they were slow as shit. Yet Mrs. Bernice was one of the sweetest women you would ever meet—a God-fearing women always talking in Scripture about life or Christ. She never had a bad thing to say about anybody, always uplifting people, and putting others before herself. Mr. Barren was just crazy. He was always talking about war guns because he was a vet and walking back and forth to the bar all day long—funny-talking, fast-walking motherfucker. Then you had Stephanie, mother of Nardo's baby, who was staying at the house too right along with Nardo's brothers: Baseball and Tayvon plus a slew of cousins; when every family was in need, it was nothing to Mom. Yeah that's what they called them: the Barrens.

Yo grabbed Zee with the retarded strength, both hands on his jacket, pulling Zee down to the ground. Maybe he just wanted Zee to embrace him. He was crying and shit, fire trucks wailing on the way to the scene.

"Fuck happen, Yo?" Zee asked.

"Yo, she looks like a ghost, a ghost dawg," Nardo replied.

"Fuck iz you talking 'bout, Nard!" Zee said.

"Man-bro, she looked like a spirit in the window," Nardo replied.

"Where are the babies, Nardo?" Zee asked.

"Boo and Kell were upstairs with Mom," Nardo replied.

Right then, Zee just snapped, "Why the fuck you out here crying an shit, not doing shit?" Zee said.

By this time, the house was blazing. Comrades were already on the scene as usually before any emergency response, leading them on a heroic tip. Without a thought, out of nowhere, G-dawg drunk ass kicked at the front door. Over hearing Zee's conversation with Nardo, G-dawg felt he should be the one taking the initiative. Now all the homeys were thinking about where the children were. Here comes the dumb shit: Nardo, Zee, and G-dawg tried to kick the front door in. Now these fools knew little about fire, like only the things that were shown on television. Bland to the fact of back draft, these idiots kicked the door in. A hard, sad lesson to be learned. How serious the elements of nurture were in life. As soon as Nardo and G-dawg kicked the door in, it was like a dragon caught his breath. The air gave the fire life; it jumped straight out on them. Zee watched in awe as the flames roll up back into the house only to forum a tornado of fire through the hall of the house up to the stairs. Just then, the windows upstairs busted. Comrades fell back feeling defeated with hands in the air from shattered glass, scourge from the draft.

G-dawg was thinking to himself there was nothing no one can do.

Zee just shook his head, mumbling, "Real life, real life."

Everybody was yelling while some were jumping on the blame game. Not that it's going to change anything. Capone and them just felt helpless, and that was never their way.

"Yo, how the fuck you get out an leave your babies in that bitch?" Zee asked.

"This nigga was talking 'bout the fire started in the back of the basement. I asked him how the fuck he got out? Told me he kicked the front basement window out and that the fire had already engulfed the basement steps," Chief said.

Even though it's an old house, and everything nigga's still drilling him about leaving them babies in that house.

"There's no way in hell I'm leaving my babies in a burning house. Don't give a fuck if I had to go through hell and back. Fuck, that shit! Walk through fire, nigga, and I mean that shit literally," G-dawg said.

"Nardo, you honestly don't believe that there was nothing you could have done. You should have kicked the door in when you first came out. What thee fuck! Anything, something nigga don't know, just know I wouldn't have left my babies in there. I'm brun up too!" Zee said.

Zee looked at this man with eyes of fire while his household was up in flames. One had to consider himself because the look on Nardo's face was blank. It was indescribable how loss of emotion was shown in him. Nardo was just sitting there taking all the blame for his sorrows. Comrades had to get the hell away from Nardo; things were just too sad. By this time, the whole block was outside, and someone else could comfort Nardo slow ass. Zee turned to Loco with a face of dismay, just shaking his head.

"Where are the kids?" Loco said.

"In the house," Zee replied softly.

"The house!" Loco yelled out real loud. "That bitch up in flames; say it's not so?" Loco said.

"It's so," Zee said.

"Why the fuck y'all ain't get them children out that house? Y'all, fuck you mean, y'all? Zee asked.

"I just got up here right before you, nigga. The house was already up in smoke when we came up here." Zee said.

"Man, I pray that them babies are not in there," Loco said.

"Where did G-dawg go?" Zee asked.

Zee looked around, and chaos was everywhere—fire marshal, police, news, etc. People were hanging around just to catch a glimpse of the commotion. Now the law wanted order, so they began to tape off the block. Nigga's wouldn't trying hear none of that. So, of course, they got into an argument with the authorities. So much tension was in the air, and everybody wanted to know the deal now that the fire is out.

The marshal, firefighters, and police all gather together talking. El-Capone and them all knew what the conversation was about. They were just waiting on the authorities to confirm their thoughts to at least bring some type of claim or peace among them. The block was already in an uproar, and you could see that the authorities didn't want no static (no trouble). Zee never did like an audience; anyway, it's not about Zee at this time. Even though one here, to the end, observe as all chums fade away in the wind. Neither by himself did he create this way. And no one else will be able to show you the Hill this way. Please forgive this pen because of one arrogance: this fire just has one devil bent.

Little body bags, little body bags, two little body bags through the alley they bring them out like trash. Do the math; here comes another bag mom's toe tag. A tragedy that's so grim. The reason behind one's mind spinning.

Nardo's cigarette hanging from his lips like he knows no good. There's no need in comforting him because there's more to tell as brothers and sisters yell.

The scene began to fade while the firemen walked the bodies up the alley toward Montford Avenue. Zee just looked at gaze, and his view was getting bleary. There were tears from his eyes, yet his face was dry. Take you on another ride, different phases jumped on to a different stage. So we fade. Let's fade away, away…

CHAPTER 5

Proceed with Caution

A FADED SCENE to some Caucasian lady in the same alley. Matter of fact, she was right in the middle of the street by the alley. Now if you don't know, some may say Port Street is a narrow block. The Hill was like an alley street. Killer Hill was the field where they did what they willed. Some may say they kill for the thrill. "Never mind all that." Now Zee was in the block arguing with some white lady. She told him dope and changed her mind to coke.

"See, that's that dumb ass shit! You told me one thing, now you on some other shit (*wondering in his mind*). Sales know drug dealers hate when they do this shit, yet they still do it. So I run and get you this shit, and now you want a nigga to make another trip. This the type of shit have a nigga knocked off," Zee said.

Just as the words were coming out of Zee's mouth, Jhon-Jhon (police) rode past them on Jefferson Street. Zee and the Caucasian fiend looking right at them rode by while his hand was out and her hand received. "Lord, have mercy; these whore's backing up," Zee said to himself while he and the fiend got stuck just looking dumbfounded at the police.

Here's how this scenario played out: They began to back up to turn into the block. Zee and the sale just watching the law ran straight down on them. It was like they were stuck and caught with their hands in the cookie jar, and the police just hit the lights. Maybe, it could have been that Jhon-Jhon rode past them first. Peeling backward tire's screeching, Zee was frozen until the police tried to whip into that narrow block. The dickheads ran into the curb, and when they hit that curb, it was like red light, green light, freeze tag, and all. Zee took off, and his silly ass fell as soon as he stepped foot in the alley. He didn't even notice the pill he dropped right along with the ten-dollar bill laying in the alley.

The bounce of a ball was how Zee hit the ground and got up again. Zee ran to his left into the yard of the double does. That is what niggas called those two houses. It was two houses connected together on the inside. Mr. Barry, G-dawg's baby mother's father, used to own them, and he knocked out the dining room's wall. You could only enter the double bando's from one of the house's basement doors. The back door is also off on the other bando, but it has no step with a rotted porch and two beams holding on for dear life. See, homeboys play the first bando where you enter from the basement door. There are all kinds of hidden spots between the two does.

"Shit!" Zee said as he glanced back, running through the basement door. The law was in his bushes (lurking, pursuing). He knew that the front of the house was boarded up. His attention really was to hide in the bandos. By that time, he ducked under the porch to get to the basement door where he had to go down about three steps while the male officer waved his female partner to go around the front. Instinct kicked in, thinking to himself, *the front of the doe's dead anyway*. So the only way out of the abandoned house now was the kitchen back door of the other house. Zee hauled his ass up the basement stairs through the dining room to the other side of the does. Zee arrived at the kitchen back door.

To his amusement, this whore was scared as Zee pilots in his mind. The whole time he was thinking about the police on his heels, this dickhead has his gun out proceeding with caution through the basement door. Zee gave it a second, maybe a minute too early then hopped out the door into the next old yard and was in the wind. The lady officer was out front, dickhead yo on his caution training into the bando while Zee ran down the split of the alleys laughing the whole time. He was wondering what was going through the police's mind in that empty vacancy because Zee definitely buss 'em up (to get away from). Zee tickled pink recalling the dumb look on the police's face entering that basement door.

CHAPTER 6

Besties

AROUND THIS TIME, Zee was living down Highlandtown on Clinton Avenue. Not going to say that one had the best state of upbringing. Even though Zee had opportunities that some of his row dawgs didn't have, they were the things that were instilled in him; his mom always had a hustle hard work ethic. You could say that the niggas on the Hill were all from good homes. G-dawg had both parents in his household. El-Capone's home was a little run-down because his people were alcoholics. And a few homeboys' moms used drugs, but regardless, all our moms were golden.

Oddly to say, individuals also had stepfathers that played major roles. Loco's brother always kept a job, and Slam's stepfather was the man. Zee's stepfather was a veteran, and Mom was always on the job. But you couldn't tell comrades anything. The hood was their family. Even now Zee didn't stay at his mom's house. He was always in the street looking for some clothes to wear because Zee has clothes scattered everywhere. After Zee finished washing his ass, the situation came to play in his mind about the police. How he would make niggas laugh at the situation that took place because nobody was around when he was being chased. He was wondering if comrades were worrying about his whereabouts. He was thinking about chilling until the sun goes down or at least 'til the police change shift. Plus, they had to be rookies because Zee never saw them before.

Anyway, Zee had to go home to grab the hammer (gun). Never leave home without it, and for some reason, something said to take the biscuit (gun). He was always taking heed to his intuition knowing that it is God talking to him. Rather be judged by twelve than carried by six, rather do a five-year bit before one in a six-feet ditch. That was just the street code and rules that help one get by. Even though there was always a ratchet (gun) on deck in the block, he looked out back before he leaves the house for a different shirt on the line.

Where the hell did this neo orange bike come from in the yard? Zee pondered to himself.

Never mind all that. This was the ticket up the way. In his mind, he would grab the bike from out back also taking Besties a 357 Mag bulk built rubber grip with a red tip. That motherfucker was special to him; she was Zee's baby. He began banging (doing something) up the way on that bright ass bike, war ready, when he ran into Murder. (That was the name of this dude from New York; come to find out.) So Zee was riding up Fayette Street.

Now this idiot had to be on the most silly shit in the city. Murder don't know he'd done rolled up on one of Baltimore's most thuggish. One couldn't begin to say what type of dudes in the city Murder was hanging around. Now he has the right one baby, like one says. Look right! (pay attention, about to tell a story). Zee was cooling on the bike, minding his business. This clown on a bike too was coming in the opposite direction. For some reason, they locked eyes, then this fool replied.

"Fuck is you looking at nigga!" Murder said.

"You whore!" Zee replied back.

They continued to roll by one another, just ice grilling (mugging) each other. The next thing you know, this silly ass nigga, Murder, began to buck a U-turn. Zee made a right on to Lakewood ending up in the middle of the intersection right across the street from the school Zee used to attend. Murder followed him into the median. Now Zee felt some type of way thinking this nigga must be strapped.

Bout to do this nigga in was running all through Zee's mind.

Without a hint of hesitation, Zee wiped out Besties and began letting loose. Banging off on Murder, he threw about five of them, hot ones at him, trying to kill his dumb ass. Murder jumped off the bike trying to get outa there. Notice how his shirt protruded off him, looking like it went straight through.

Zee said, "Yeah, hit his whore ass." As Zee put the biscuit (gun) back in his crotch, it burned all hell out of his leg. So Zee gave a glance around and saw some trippy shit. Directly behind Zee was a big statue of a soldier with a gun. "Man, ah, nigga, get outa there. Shit was just too hot, neo bike hit and all."

Then as soon as Zee approached forty (which was Orleans), the police on Glover, the next street over, just knew they had to hear that chaos. Zee hit Jefferson Street and took it all the way up the hill looking like a cucumber, green as a whore on a bright-orange bike rolling up on the block, and niggas out. Zee instantly gained the power, the juice, some type of enjoyment like he was the man or something. He slammed the bike down in the alley as he was getting off it. Nigga had seen that it was something in him; they just couldn't put the hand on it.

"Yo!" Zee had his arms stiff straight down, swinging them side to side while he took silly strides toward comrades. "Why, I just had to burn this fool up!" Zee said.

"Yeah, Son, we just heard that shit. That was you?" Chief asked.

Zee ran over to Loco's yard to put the biscuit up. For some reason, El-Capone went to check the shells in the biscuit. Like a nigga was lying or something, Capone was just always on some other shit. Now Zee, on his shit, couldn't tell him nothing about the clout.

"I say right, Cuz, roll down there and see wit it do. See if yo dead cause I know I hit him," Zee said.

Zee started to explain the situation to his comrades.

"Hell no! My nigga don't take that bright ass bike. That's the one I was on," Zee said real quick. "Yeah, Yo, this nigga was silly than a motherfucker. Talking 'bout what I'm looking at."

Smoking and joking about how he rides gives him a feeling of some type of pride. When dawg came up the hill, he was talking about how fuck up Murder was down there.

"Fuck up, yo, dead down that bitch?" Zee asked.

"Nah, but he's most definitely on the half down that bitch," El-Capone replied.

"Told y'all! I tried to kill that whore down there. Bitch azz nigga, I don't know what the fuck be going through these niggas minds these days," Zee said.

CHAPTER 7

Relapse

NIGGAS BANGING ON to the next day, 24/7; niggas in the hood, knock on wood where partners say it's all good. It never was a dull moment on the Hill, and someone stayed on deck, always on point. They were ahead of their time; there were no other units as such in the city. Their way was unique; it was just the way, and they made it that way. Anyway, dawgs out her thuggin' on the Hill, mayhem at every corner. From Milton Avenue up to Montford with Port Street, the alley street in the middle. This was considered to be the perimeter of the Hill, also Jefferson down to forty, which was Orleans.

See, we have the smokers and the drinkers, and this was how comrades were segregated. The drinkers didn't want shit! All they wanted was to leech off the smokers and cause beef (trouble). Zee was the chief smoker (a.k.a. General) and stayed focused on the paper (money). And better believe it, Zee was getting to the bag. And there were only a few smokers to be exact: Loco, Si, Zee, Chief, and Mark; five came later, and V was down for whatever.

Now the rest of the dawgs stayed on some bullshit, always dragging another homeboy with them. Now envy showed its face in the block. Si and Zee were getting to it (getting money). Every time these two linked up, it be on and popping. They always got to the bag, and that's a whole other chapter. This is about how your so-called homeboys always trying to destroy what a nigga builds.

Si and DE started arguing over a sale. Before you know it, DE just knocked the fiend straight out. And that was how it all started! They even had Zee trying to knock junkies out. Idiots! It was all a game on the Hill. Dawgs didn't give a fuck about the money; it was just another way to knock the flow. Plus, niggas got into a whole bunch of nonsense about putting their hands on people. Yet nobody could content with the Hill; comrades were too much.

"Bet you can't knock him out," With a smile on his face, Zee said while he and DE were watching a three-hundred-pound fiend walked up the block to cop. Matter of fact, if one could remember, Zee and DE were working together around this time (speaking of the times) before one jumped the gun!

"We'll catch back up to this knocking-people-out shit."

CHAPTER 8

Big Cuz

MUST PUT Y'ALL up on the game about the reign of Miles.

"Gonna let me hold the car, Cuz?" Zee said.

Big Cuz was laughing and dangling the keys to the Audi 5000 in Zee's face. Zee snatched them motherfuckers and was in the wind through the alley with nothing but gas on his chest (wanting to joy-ride). Now Cuz was an easy three-hundred-pounds, and you will be amazed how fast his big ass moves. He never gives chase though. Why the fuck Zee took that man shit? Then on top of it with no Ls (license) and to make matters worse, Zee grabbed his brother with the license like he was doing something slick. Yeah, Bro and Zee were joyriding for a few. Young and dumb, they didn't know the whole time guns, and nothing but drugs in the car. Man! Big Cuz caved Zee's whole chest in; all wind came up out of Zee. Now Zee was all fucked up and couldn't breathe and some more shit.

The thing that hurt the most was his pride; he thought the situation was all jokes and games While the whole block laughed at his silly ass. "Yo shake that shit off, man up," Zee told himself. He was thinking about getting a stick or something because this dude was really big. Zee was pondering, *Like what the fuck that's gonna do. Done seen this nigga work, done watch this nigga run through whole family's 4x4 and all.*

"Damn Cuz, right," Zee said to himself. Zee was on some super moron shit. Speaking of that drug life, niggas were knocking (getting money) on the block. Now Big Cuz was not with outsiders getting money in the block. Even though these niggas live in the block, it was just the principle that they were not from around the way. Nobody knew Detroit and Dre or where the fuck they come from been mentioned so many times, especially to their whore asses.

Plus, when Big Cuz first came home and was just chilling at his aunt's house in the block, Dawn, his girl cousin, got into a family feud with Dre's sister which, in turn, turned out to be Detroit's old lady. She was a hideous thing, always wanting to fight. It was just that girl demeanor; she was anything, Her short wide body, bifocal wearing ass. Anyway they get to arguing about something. Then all you know was Miles (a.k.a. Big Cuz) hopping up off the steps. This incident was so vivid like it happened yesterday because the altercation was kind of amusing in a way.

Now we all know Big Cuz, like three hundred plus, jumped up off the steps running straight to the situation teeing off (hitting) on the bitch. He ran down on that woman and gave her a death blow. She buckled at the knees, believing he hit her in the ribs somewhere. He slid on her and gave her two upper cuts to the body. She ate the two upper cuts and gave us two bunny hops right along with a few grunts that stunned the onlookers. Dawg was dying laughing on the block. El-Capone had tears in his eyes imitating the bunny hops while holding his stomach. Now in Zee's mind, *He like damn Cuz; she's a woman.*

Big Cuz didn't give a fuck about none of that. Family always came first no matter what. Looking at it—Detroit's girl, Dre's sister—and them, whores didn't do anything. Back to the matter at hand, with these whore ass clowns, both of these niggas were on some pity whore shit. The topic at hand was these dudes were always trying to steal off the block. They stayed asking dawgs questions about the Hill. One can hear Dre or Detroit saying, "What y'all got, dope, rock, or coke? What size viles niggas be putting their shit in?" Sneak dissing (talking behind your back) all day long trying to fox (investigate, betrayal) someone out.

Walking action round the corner and all like dawgs don't know what they're doing. Big Cuz really didn't give a fuck; it was that these dudes stayed scheming. For instance, one day, Detroit had some individuals on the block. Comrades didn't know these dudes from a can of paint. Later, Miles found out they were from Greenmont. So niggas played right into Dre's and Detroit's hands.

"Why the fuck them two bitches keep looking up here at me talking to them niggas?" Big Cuz asked.

"Man, those whores don't want no static for real!" Chief said.

"See, there they go again; these whores, they were on some shit. They know they don't want none of this. Man, fuck it! Get 'em y'all," Big Cuz said.

When Miles say go, niggas were already gone.

Slam was rolling with the rush (down for anything), and Zee was right with him. Big Cuz always did things himself. So when he put dawgs on them, they were delighted to do so. Zee grabbed Besties from Loco's porch. Slam had a thirty-eight special. Them niggas must have felt something. So the dudes with Detroit and Dre started walking to their car. Their car was parked on the curb down by the alley at Orleans. Like one says, the Hill is a side street, a little alley block. So the car was on the curb so other cars could pass by. Meanwhile Zee and Slam were running down the back alley opposite of their car. Here, these fools go. Zee and Slam approached the split in the alley, jumping out blasting. Then they didn't hit anything, and comrades were watching as paint and brick fell from the wall. Plus, Slam and Zee were about the distance of a half of a block, maybe a quarter of a block.

"Fuck it!" Big Cuz yelled.

Niggas were just sending a message, but if comrades only knew, maybe, Cuz would have done things a different way. Man, them dudes came back through like a whirlwind. Momma always said, "Boy, there's someone out there time enough for your ass."

Couldn't tell the Hill nothing they was that, and that was that. Hell yeah, them Greenmount dudes came through a couple times spot-checking. Dawgs were out dumbing but always ready to meet 'em. We all stayed strapped (carrying guns); plus, Big Cuz knew those brothers were coming.

CHAPTER 9

That! (Anything Pertaining to Subject)

A FEW NIGHTS passed by as Zee was on his way in the house, actually, his baby mom's house which was about a block or two away from the Hill. Soon as Zee came through the door, every bit of ninety shots rang out.

"Damn! I know somebody dead, all that hammering (gun shots)," Zee said.

Not thinking at all about the situation around the way, Gem was happy he just made it home safe in the nick of time. Grabbing and tugging on Zee, Gem was pulling him into the house while the shots were still echoing through the hood. Zee peeped out the vestibule of the door giving Gem a little resistance.

He just stared in the air when Gem asked, "What are you doing?"

He turned and locked eyes with her for a moment, relinquishing control over to her dragging him into the house. Before you know it, Zee and the mother of his children all booed up. Matter of fact, they didn't even have any children at the time. Zee grabbed that phat juicy ass on this woman's body; Lord, have mercy. Gem's frame around this era was deadly; really, she was that!

On top of all that, Gem was unique. So flexible, she could lose weight, get phat, back to skinny with a fat ass the whole while. She kept a wonderful waist, long legs thick to the hips with feet so sweet. Even to this day, Gem's chest is to be desired. Plus, her lips, Zee was trying to decide which ones should he kiss? He threw Gem's thighs up on his shoulder while he's kneeling down in front of the bed. He began sucking and kissing softly on that click, twirling his tongue around while he sucked then kissed. He did this over and over again. Zee gave a glance up, *What a magnificent frame* was running through his brain.

Gently laying her leg down as he raised the other on his shoulder, I view of Gem's breast and stomach on her back with that hip out to match made Zee want to devour that. He slid down, nibbling lightly and sucking Gem's nipple's back and forth on each one. He couldn't get enough trying to swallow a whole breast. Her mound was just too much; he slid his tongue down to the lips, kissing and sucking that twat only to flip her ass over and eat it from the back. He opened Gem's ass up, and with his tongue, he tickled her twat.

Admiring while palming that ass, *Such a masterpiece* he thought to himself, only wanting to eat her up, so he stuck his tongue right in her hole, hit it three times in and out; while coming out, he was sucking on the bottom of her back hole, tongue pounding that heresy highway and sliding his tongue all around the sides of that entrance. He dived back in 'till he was just about to lose his wind. *That's so wild how this woman tastes so scrumptious* was running through Zee's mind. He just had to have her because he was enraptured by her essence. Gem was more of a woman than Zee could have imagined.

Taking back control of the situation, Zee began to smash, twat so wet he almost crashed. He had to slow down, too much woman to enjoy, slowly grinding around and around in a circle motion. Zee grabbed Gem's hair and told her to look back at him. He looked at her in the eyes then started pounding even harder. Thanking the heavens for such a wonderful ass, he spread it wide open while he hit it in a down position. He took his dick for a ride on the other side, put his thumb in her butt, continuing to pump. Zee had her by the waist from her back shoulder; with his hand, Zee gave her body a trace.

Quickly, he pulled his sword out and smacked it in the crack of her buns, caressing a gift from heaven while just popping the tip of his muscle in and out that twat. He smacked Gem in the middle of her bun again with his wood. It was loud and sloppy, making it easier to slide his muscle in her caramel sundae, for that's what it tasted like to Zee anyhow with a little whipped cream.

Slowly, his motion, as he winded his wrench, Gem grabbed the front of his thigh, trying to stop him from penetrating all the way. Zee had her by his dick beater at the waist. Damn, he's halfway in while watching the bay start to swim. She threw it back like she's that. *This bitch in it to win, she wants it all in*, thinking to himself. He was all in juices in her ass blend.

Out of breath, he had nothing left. Gem turned around and lay on his chest. One thing you can say about Zee: that yo a freak. Plus, by Gem being so bad, it was nothing for Zee to get back in the line. Gem knew this, rubbing Zee's stomach playing with his sword. She put his semi love muscle in her mouth, and it instantly swelled up. His freak ass back because Zee adores Gem's knowledge. Deep throat, loving it when she choked and how it poked her throat.

Sculpturing that wood like a masterpiece, she gave a little choke from some pokes. There's some spit to lick it all over that stick. Just to devour it, the whore almost took Zee's soul. *How the hell is she making that moaning sound while gasping and laughing. Then this bitch got tears in her eyes*, Zee was delighted in his mind. He couldn't take it anymore, so he had to grab her to stop and kiss her blessed lips. Gem cherished the love and fell right back in line to swallow the whole nine.

When the news caught Zee's attention, the one thing he didn't want to believe was on TV. It was the block, and four people had just been shot. Zee pulled Gem up, making sure it was around the way. Man! Zee knew the block plus that look like Loco's coat on the ground. He's glued to the television like crazy. Zee's body languished giving off a go mode. Gem felt the vibe trying to hold him back from his ride. Zee got in the wind, time to spin the bend.

CHAPTER 10

Consequences of Rush

The Hill was superhot, so Zee was definitely putting that thing up. He threw the tool (gun) in another bandomanin around the corner. Zee came upon the block just to be derailed by Capone, Chief, and G-dawg walking the perimeter. They were with who else but Nardo. See, you know Nardo lives in the block, so he's like eyewitness news. Never has one seen a nigga so frantic and anxious to tell a motherfucker what happened. (Don't get it twisted; this is the reign of Big Cuz before Mrs. Bernice's house burned down.) This donkey is too dramatic; just listen to him.

"Loco dead, Yo! They just kept shooting him on the ground," Nardo said.

"Kept! Fuck iz you talking 'bout B? How the fuck you set here an' say some ill shit like that. When we all stay nappy (carrying guns)," Chief said.

"Slam had gotten hit, an' I ran into him coming out the hole (alley), and I dragged him into the house," Nardo said.

"So you mean to tell me that you helping a dawg running through the alley while watching Loco getting blown up!" Chief said.

"You could have at least thrown a couple at they ass, get them nigga's up off him," El-Capone said.

"You think Yo dead?" G-dawg asked.

Chief sags his head down, shaking his head with something like a grin with his expression. Die hard Wu Tang fan, Chief was really trying to hold it together tripping off of G-dawg. Thinking about a Wu track when dude was saying, "Is, he dead?"

"Yeah Yo, feather were everywhere from his coat. It looked like it was snowing out. Man, they shoot him like ten times!" Nardo said.

Yeah, they tried to put Loco in the grave, but Loco came up out of that shit. They put nine holes in him then again eighteen because the bullets went straight through. Maybe it was the era because, around this time, everybody was wearing big goose coats. That coat probably saved his skinny ass, but really, the Lord had mercy on him. Ms. Toya, who was Loco's soon to be baby's mother, was also hit twice and once in the face. Slam big unorthodox ass caught a slug (been shot). Plus, Ms. Mandy was hit in the leg. EL-Capone, on his dumb shit, was talking about Ms. Mandy got hit signifying.

"Who the fuck hear shots and run to the corner?" El-Capone asked.

"I just don't want none of y'all to get hurt," Ms. Mandy said.

"You rather get hurt instead, huh?" sarcastically speaking, El-Capone asked.

"That's right, baby! I love y'all and don't want to see nothing happened to none of y'all." Ms. Mandy said.

"You love that coke, thinking or hoping a nigga gonna give you a pill for telling what happened," El-Capone said.

Everybody was laughing like hyenas; she was all bandaged up and some more shit sitting on the front of her house. Praise be to the force (God) that nobody died. Nigga's spin the bin a couple of times about that shit. Even though comrades didn't know who was who and who to look for.

Now Big Cuz did catch up with Detroit one day on Greenmount and slammed him on his head. Dawgs were a little satisfied with that. Some things were just ironic like that in the hood. Comrades definitely learn from each o'her's mistakes. You had to take the bitter with the sweet hanging on the Hill. One could hear Capone now.

"I don't give a fuck if my dawg wrong or right! I'm still rolling wit rush 'cause that's our unite." Comrades on the Hill, we were each other's fathers and brothers, and we lived by the codes of the street. Just to die by not following them. For there was no one above all of us because we were in perfect union with the way.

CHAPTER 11

The Conversation

"Come on now! Hell no!" Zee and Chief were going back and forth in disbelief at the sight at hand.

"What thee fuck!" Chief stated out loud.

While he and Zee were laughing, they were on a serious note. Damn it! Whole block's face dropped looking at Big Cuz and Nardo. Now Big Cuz was that! Wouldn't want to say nobody, but one had yet to see anyone play with him. Big Cuz, he could do that and get away with it. This nigga Nardo just fucked the whole show up following suit. Nardo was the real kind of fuck boy. These dudes, man, fuck it, just gonna let it out because nowadays, everybody was playing with it. Big Cuz dyed his hair blond and Nardo right behind him. Now back then, around 93–94 shit like that was not done. Even now, all you can say about Big Cuz is that he was ahead of his time. Comrades from the block was asking Zee what the fuck was wrong with your cousin. Don't know who because things were said. Like them niggas letting the money go to their head.

"Look at fuck boy number 1, he suspect on the real; he'll suck a nigga off if he tell him," El-Capone said.

None of that didn't matter; niggas were getting to that papper, Big Cuz had everybody up on the block. Now Zee was like 17–18 and was charging up (getting money).

"Let me grab this action coming up, Zee?" Chief asked.

"Man, what, you know I don't give a fuck about no play," Zee said.

"Nah, son, never like that. You just know how they always want your stuff," Chief said.

"Go ahead, player; I just hit an eight sale," Zee said.

Chief ran into the bando to grab a few more pills for the fiend. He came out shaking his head with a smirk on his face.

"Zee (*thinking*), what!"

"What happened Yo? You hit the sale? What, she only got one?" Zee asked.

"Nah, she got five of them. That's why I had to run up in the shack. I only had two of them on me. The thing is, your boy is up in there with some pipe head. Mama looks all right too with her little hooker outfit on and all," Chief said.

Zee gave a silly laugh then said, "Who is it in there?"

"I don't know the whore, never seen this fiend before."

"No, ass, I'm talking 'bout which one of us in there."

"Fuck you, though you would know anyway. Who else but Loco's no pussy getting ass. Keep running off with junkies," Chief said.

By this time, G-dawg rolled up the block talking about.

"Y'all seen Loco scary ass?" G-dawg asked.

He had a fresh 40 oz. in his hand as usual. Now Zee and Chief want to laugh and let Loco's game out. They just motioned their heads toward the shack. Wanting G-dawg to run down on Loco on his fiend shit. Now the way G-dawg ran up the steps with that grin on his face, he must have known what was going down. So a few minutes went by, and here, this nigga go.

"She looked all right, Yo?" Zee asked.

"There you go on your silly shit, told you she was okay," Chief said.

"Nah, I wanted to wait 'till she comes out and see her but them niggas got the bitch hostage," Zee said.

"Yeah, tell a nigga anything," Chief said.

"Fuck it! I'll go check her out for myself. These niggas in the basement," Zee said to Chief.

While motioning Chief to follow him down the basement, they slid down on their ass, and he wasn't lying. Auntie was cut up (nice body) for a fiend a nigga means. See, she must have just gotten off the steps (new too) when one of them just started getting high. Think about it, hustlers love to get them when they first get turned out before they roam through the town getting around. Shit, her body was really that though; you couldn't take that from her. Give it a minute or two, and that stem (smoke pipe) will fix all that. Now what killed it was the one piece she had on; auntie was really wearing her little outfit. Next thing you know, here comes El-Capone and Snot down the steps.

"Fuck y'all niggas up too in this bitch?" El-Capone said.

"Bout to get some head from this bitch," Loco said.

"Didn't you already go?" Zee said.

"Yeah, but she's that! I mean doom blazing," Loco said.

"Bet she is down here smoking up all your coke," Zee said.

This nigga Snot a hawk, straight rush the bathroom door pulled his pants down and throw his wood in the fiend's mouth.

"Damn! Fuck'z up wit you Dawg? Nigga I was next!" G-dawg said.

"O-ya Yo, it's mad action out that bitch," El-Capone said.

G-dawg fell right for the bait; El-Capone was trying to get in and out. G-dawg jumped straight on it, guessing by G knowing everybody in the house, he could get the jump on the action. Dawgs running the trick now, all types of flips and switches. I mean they were really punishing this lady. Having their way with her, she made a little fuss here and there. Dawgs were doing what they want to do to the slut, and in a way, she loved it. Now around the time G-dawg came back, Snot, El-Capone, and Loco were on their way out the door. Zee and Chief rolled up some fire, smoking and joking. So this was the kicker: bitch smoking coke like a chummy. G-dawg was really trying to go now, and she was not paying him any mind. G-dawg was watching this woman fumble with about six pills in her little pouch then came to find out G was the one who brought her around the way.

"Come on, baby, what are you doing?" G-dawg asked.

"Hold up, honey, let me finish this," One Piece said.

She was on her geek shit now, keep looking out the basement window. Now G-dawg was mad as a bitch in heat. Chief passed G the blunt attempting to calm his nerves, he was still sipping the same 40 oz. G-dawg hit the blunt a couple of times then gave it to Zee. Soon, as G-dawg passed the blunt, he snatched all hell out of her coke-smoking ass. On his Snot shit now, he was whipping his dick out trying to force it in the whore's mouth.

"Give me a second huh, I'm just finishing this up. Plus, my jaws are sore, and I'm thirsty as shit. Let me hit that drink G?" One Piece said.

Chief begins thinking to himself, *This bitch done fuck up now and asked G-dawg to hit the drink after she just ate the whole Hill up.*

To make matters even worse, G-dawg, the one that brought her around the way (neighborhood, where you hang), plus didn't get no head. You could see it all over G's face, about to bust the bitch head. All of a sudden, G-dawg cocked his arm back with the 40 oz., ready to slap all the shit out the crackhead. Chief saw it coming and grabbed G-dawg's arm real quick.

"Yo fuck is you doing?"

"Nah Yo! This bitch playing with me. I found her in the first place; she already knew wit it was," G-dawg said.

G-dawg mad as hell, he snatched away from Chief and, on his way up the steps, picked up an old pager then hurled it straight at her head. Chief and Zee ain't no more good; the way this knot grew on this lady's forehead was like a cartoon. Chief and Zee looked like Cube and Smokey on *Friday Damn*! Chief balled up on Zee's shoulder with his arms up to his face trying to hide his laughter. They stumbled over each other, knocking any and everything over, packing all types of jokes. Never had one seen a knot protrude off a person's head like this. Top it off, her high most definitely gone now. Just know, G-dawg blew her buzz with that blow. Best believe she was trying to go again, knot and all. Man! Dawgs left that whore where she stood. Okay, big cappin (lying), Zee tried his hand because the doom was that. But he just couldn't do it because her head was on half. Once that knot on her forehead touched Zee's stomach, he began laughing and pulled his sword out her mouth. Comrades outside straight-geeking, telling G-dawg about the knot on the bitch head. He didn't give a fuck; he felt like that crackhead whore deserved it.

(Slam if you're reading this which one knows you will. You and I know what's going on. Don't know why one switches you with G-dawg, but everything has its reason. Ponder on that because one knows you remember that episode.)

CHAPTER 12

Miles

ALL WAS WELL in the hood; before you know it Big Cuz banged around the corner, him and Loco. Loco must have ran into him coming up the hill because Loco was just in the block. The look in Big Cuz's eyes was fury.

"Yo, these niggas just tried me down the hill! I'm down there fighting with 'bout five niggas on me, fucking with Mia..."

(Vicarious mind state)

"Where at cousin?" Chief asked.

"We were down in Highland Town fighting, but them niggas be chilling up on Bond and Perston. They think a nigga don't know," Big Cuz said.

Say no more, niggas began to suit up. Loco grabbed hulk built, rubber grip, with the red tip. Chief had this young ass tre deuce (.32 caliber) but effective. G-dawg bangging a three-eighty (.380 caliber) with a lemon squeeze. As El-Capone hosted the cock and popped a 44 Mag, niggas came equipped with hoods, gloves, and masks. El-Capone always liked to get rid of the tools (guns). For this reason, someone designed a plan for one of the young puppies to meet them on a bike with a book bag on and by the park alley. Flip script now four masks down in the latest ghetto ride. Plus, they were all high, which means someone was gonna die.

"Don't be going down, hear me now, playing with these bitches! Oh yeah, make sure y'all get the one with the moe on his face," Big Cuz said.

Hopping out the car all to the same beat. Synchronized their stride size as they booped up the street. Silence among them not a peep. Before niggas even bend the corner. Loco started letting off, bodies on bikes dropping. Chief catches him to the ground continually popping. El-Capone was at chase with the long nose 44 Mag trying to walk this one dude down. Taking small strides in and out of Bond Street, moving while aiming, trying to lay him down. But the sound of that 44 rang through the whole town. G-dawg was stiff as a whore with the lemon squeeze. He didn't even lick a shot like he didn't know how to work the squeeze; talking about it wouldn't cock. Through all the mayhem, all it would have taken was a glimpse to the side. Niggas would have seen Yo with the moe. This whore balled up ducking in the corner of the steps, terrified the whole time.

Soon, as dawgs hit the corner, one just jumped the gun and started booming on everybody in sight. While this dude with the moe right there was ducking down on the wall at the first house. (If he was a snake, he would have bitten niggas.) Good thing Moe Yo wasn't stripped; he just didn't move not an inch, and he just stayed balled up in that corner. Chief all banged out, so he got loose; comrades followed suit. Chief and Loco in the wind, El-Capone was still cutting loose on the cock and pop tip. G-dawg was still holding ground fumbling with the lemon. Dawgs all hit the same alley and split ways running through. Loco came upon the dude El-Capone was trying to gun down. Loco's mission now was to get to the drop-off spot. It was kind of slick in a way but dumb as a brick plan for real. The drop-off plan worked, and that was all that mattered.

Loco made his way to the spot, and as soon as he hit the corner, he saw one of the dawgs making his drop. Before you knew it, another comrade came through the alley throwing the biscuit (gun) in the bag and kept it pushing. Finally, Loco got to the drop; he about faced and hit the opposite direction of the first two thugs. Loco saw G-dawg's drunk ass from his peripheral vision coming up the park alley last. Comrades all met up on the block and started rolling up blunts and cracking drinks showing love (pouring out liquor). While dawgs were smoking and drinking, a dude from up that way rode through the block alley on a bike. Everybody was just looking at each other like what the fuck was that about. Next thing you know, this nigga was licking off shots from Jefferson Street.

"He's on some lame ass shit. Don't know why he just didn't bang on niggas when he came through the alley the first time. His results would have been better," Zee replied.

Consequently, V did get caught in the leg by a piece of railing from the bullet ricochet.

"I'm going to kill that little whore when I catch him," V said.

So a few days pass by when Capone came to tell comrades.

"Yo, they locking up Big Miles around 7-11 now," El-Capone said.

"Shit! For what?" Zee said.

"How the fuck was I supposed to know!" El-Capone said.

To put it in a cell, Big Miles went down for that situation. They gave Big Miles eighty years for that incident, and he didn't pull a trigger. The courts labeled him as a menace to society. For he was the one who sent individuals to do his dirty work. Don't think this is the end of Miles as the phoenix rises from the ashes. Zee in it all alone now. He has his dawgs, his so-called day ones. Yet he knew that his family, by blood, had his best interest at heart. Straight thuggin', balling on these suckers in this city. Nobody wanted to get in the Hill path; everybody knew niggas on the Hill were foolish. Yet Big Miles did leave Zee with a test for that dough, which in turn would keep him away from the foolishness and focus on the chase for the paper.

CHAPTER 13

Pussy Be the Reason

After the fall of Miles, things became karma in the hood. One thing after another, it wouldn't be this, then it would be that. Then Face came home and, bro, was definitely about that paper. El-Capone and Face were row dawgs, the real kind. See, Comrades come and go in the hood, and El-Capone was knocked off around this time. So when Face hit the block, he and Zee clicked straight like that. Face was known to be serious when it came to the Hill. Dawgs didn't really know any plugs (supplier), and with no source, the way was in shambles. By El-Capone being pinched (getting locked up), individuals were on other things while some were on some dumb crap. So this made Face feel obligated to pave the way.

Comrades always tried to make something shake for the Hill. One hand washed the other both to the face; this is the way. Oh yeah, don't get it miscue because of Face's smooth cut, Cuz will get straight with you. Talking about zipped out type stuff, cuz go black on you. Face stayed on his slick shit always fresh, running through all the mopheads. Cuz was thug out in a different realm; he was before his time. As some may say or maybe he just knew how fast his time would fly. Guess that's why Face stayed so fly and always high. Dudes would always overlook him, and that's why Zee understood Face. Just loving the fact that one would never see his dawg coming.

Anyway, Face found the source, and Si and Zee were up at bat running the base (working drug shop). Of course, they were getting to the bag, banging straight coke (powder cocaine) too, no rock. Dawgs had never seen fiends run like this before in their life. Like really all over some coke! Let me tell you, fiends used to wait on this coke like it was heroin. Face live on Orleans Street right at the corner of Port Street. So this donkey stayed throwing packs out the window. Bro was up on his game about that currency. Si and Zee were getting paid by night plus at the end of the week. Really wasn't bad for the moment from nothing. Dawgs were selling too much coke though. Now Face cop (purchased) a little car for the hood. Little blue car they used to call it The Blue something. Check how bugged out the comrade Face was. He made the car "the Hill's fun toy." Dawgs made a game up called straight ballin.' Listen to this retarded shit; to participate, you had to run upstairs, jumped out the window, run to the car, and dawgs balled out, no stoplights, stop signs, and everything else. Doing about fifty coming up Monument Street on the one-way tip. So reckless and dangerous and none of it registered with them. I mean like where was the police because dawgs did this a few times. There were a couple of close calls with other vehicles, but the law never persuaded the blue-baller.

Now this dude named Bay-Bay, baby mother, moved in the block. Face and Bay-Bay knew each other from hustling together on Ashland Avenue. Funny talking, tall black ugly ass dude. Bay-Bay was used to getting that bag, and at some point in time, he might rob you. Things were so ill in the hood; one even saw Bay with his head in his dick (getting high). At this particular time, Bay-Bay was getting a couple of dollars. This for all the players in this so-called game, hood, or thug life. Plus, a bunch of y'all tender dudes should tune in. Women come and go; never let pussy be the reason for the bleeding. In this case, principle plays a factor, and it's always good to live by morals that are set before you. Nevertheless, the dawg flashing, so you already know Face smashing (having sex).

Now Bay-Bay was upset talking about, "We are supposed to be homeboys." Now there are codes on the street that you should live by just to die by. Man dawgs on the Hill didn't give a fuck about none of that principle crap. Face was like comrades (OG, original gangster), so it really didn't matter who he was putting the dick in. For real,

Comrades really weren't paying the situation any mind until Bay and Face had words on the block one day.

"All the shit we did together, the trenches we crawled out, like you didn't know who the fuck she was," Bay-Bay said.

"Who says I didn't?" Face asked.

"Damn, Cuz, like there's no more honor among thieves. That's some bitch's ass shit," Bay-Bay said.

"What's some bitch's ass shit? And why the fuck it got to be all like that? Face asked.

This whore was mad about the whole ordeal anyway, and this situation didn't make things any better. "Anger resides in the lap of fools" This whore sent some young punks at a dawg. They came from the alley across the street on some prayer to god hit. They had to be at least a half a block away, and luck is not the word. It was said that it was nothing more than a fate shot. That there was nothing no one could do about it. Couldn't tell that shit to Chief; he believed with all his heart that these younglings were in that alley and aimed at Face.

Now it was around the Fourth of July because everybody was running around playing like they were shot by the fireworks. Face was on the corner with DE if one was not mistaken. All of the sudden, Face started running down the block holding his chest. It was mad fireworks going off, so niggas thinking Face was on his bullshit. Chief watched Bro laughing at him until he noticed the look on his face. This was not a game; this was the real thing. Zee's face began to drop in silence. The way Face's failed didn't make sense. He was running so fast when everything just dropped. When everybody saw how Face collapsed, it put all at awe. Zee hauled tall over to see what was wrong with his comrade.

"Yo! What fuck happen?" Zee questioned, standing over top of his round (homeboy) while he held his chest breathing his last breaths. DE came from around the corner talking about.

"Yo, I think somebody shot at us from the alley," DE said.

"What alley? Y'all were on the corner," Chief asked.

"I know the whores were across Jefferson in the five hundred block of Port Street in the alley," DE said.

"Yo wit thee fuck! I know my nigga ain't dying on me. Wit thee fuck, not like this son, hell no!" Chief said.

"Face! Face! Face!" Loco yelled. "All y'all motherfucker get the fuck away from him; he need his air. Y'all back the fuck up!"

Cuz began to slip away while this nut Zee was looking at Face while he died in his eyes. Zee put his head down and started walking away. In disbelief, he knew his partner was not in that shell no more.

"Unbelievable! Bro, light was gone just like that in the bat of an eye. Yo, who the fuck did this? They died! Somebody, go get Cuz's people," Zee said.

"Already went, they not home. I think they are at work or something. That's crazy, my ace going out like this; get the keys. Face got the MAC-11 (semiauto gun) in the house," Chief said.

"We 'bout to ride 'bout this somebody's gotta die," DE said as he grabbed the keys out of Face's pocket.

Niggas began to put the pieces together to figure out the pilot behind Face. Because that shit was aimed for him. It was a few old heads on the block that dawgs were in competition with. But they played by the rules; now come to think of it, Zee and DE were ready to kill Moo-Moo.

His car was parked in the block by the Killer Hill wall. While he was in the trap getting his shit together, they went out back lurking under the steps in the yard right by his car. Shit never popped off; he was in there too long niggas went on another mission. Someone got to get it! Ride down on these little so-called thugs; the old heads said they saw running through the alley, whip straight out, only one of them was on the step. He ain't even the one killers were looking for. Yo's scared ass got outa there!

Zee was always told to never pull that thing unless you're gonna use it. Now he was standing there with the MAC-11 out, so he just like fuck it and got to rocking on him. Don't think he hit him, but they kIthe Hill was coming. Yeah, Zee let them niggas know dawgs were on to them. That Comrade knew who did that fuck shit and that Bay-Bay whore ass sent y'all. One not gonna lie, money has its way with you if you let it.

Even though elders were letting things cool off, some of the thugs weren't for none of that. Especially when El-Capone came home, it was on! Face was El day one. By Zee being next up with the connect, he just let them niggas handle that with his input on direction. Now Zee's mind was on the money. "Life goes on" as Pac said. And before this journey is over, you will understand why some are so numb to death. How it became so easy for some to take a precious light (life).

CHAPTER 14

2417 Orleans

SI AND ZEE were at the top of the food chain now. You're talking about dragging before you even knew that. Si was cutting up new outfits every day. Most of the time, bro was just redundant with it. Wiping his ass with the cash, shitting on shit. Si was an arrogant, conceited type of dude, always about that tissue (money) and did not play when it came to the paper. He was more of the negotiating one. Zee was laid back in his own little community while Si did all the networking in the world. If one may say, Si was Zee's partner on some Batman and Robin shit. As Si would say, "I'm Super-Man; you are Bat-Man." See what one mean; they bust the coke moves, and they get to the dumb dough. Si and Zee had fucked up a lot of blow running through all the dope. Not to exaggerate, they accumulated enough together that they didn't even know what they were doing.

One day, they looked up, and they had like a brick and a half, four cars, a bundle of weapons, about a hundred grams of raw, and five or six pounds of weed. Man, they fucked the money up! Guess that's what you do when it's your time, and you fuck up your turn. The house 2417 Orleans, yeah, that was the spot. This was the start of the Soul era, its uncle house, while Zee was just running up the dough. Plus, Zee figured Soul could help him with the business and all. After all, he is the one that introduced Zee to the dope game. Lenny Hymmon, that was Uncle shit! He would say in a stuttering voice, "That's my name on the dope; it's gonna sell." Soul was a made man in the city. Did one mention that Soul was in a relationship with Zee's aunt for about fifteen years? He used to always say, "Boy, I am the one who brought you your first pair of leather shoes."

It wasn't a person in the city that he didn't know. Either they knew of him or his family name. Zee was trying to bring him back into the game. Whole time, he was just laid back, saying to the plug.

"Man, just give the boy that shit!" Soul said.

Never was there a time around the way when Zee had Soul by his side, and there wasn't a way. People used to just give Soul shit out of the blue, mean like everything, guns, clothes, shoes, and dogs. Plus, let's not talk about all the drugs; whatever it was, niggas were in on it. Say right he'll get drunk and go off on you all night, cussing and fussing at everybody, no picks. Yet for Zee, their first run came to mind on Orleans because DE came into play. DE was kind of hustling with Zee. Si had got knocked off and all Soul did was dictate. Can't really say that bro was a fuck up, just a bad place, wrong time, type of individual. The wrong energy just always follow this man. Besides, the fact of him being an alcoholic doesn't help any. DE was kind of a nut, especially when he was drinking. Who doesn't have a whole other side under the influence though?

"Yo, how do you do it?" Zee asked.

"Do what?" DE replied.

"Knock people out like that," Zee said.

Zee had a smile on his face as he looked at a three-hundred-pound junkie walking up the block to cop.

"Bet you can't knock him out?" Zee replied.

"See wit (what) you gotta do is when you hit 'em through your whole body into them." DE said.

Anyway, a couple of the homeys didn't get all into that, putting their hands on people wasn't the thing. And just for the thrill of it wasn't cool even though it was amusing to observe. Now we have just been caught up from that relapse. Yeah, this was the time when Zee and DE were rolling together. You can say they were getting some currency, but DE wasn't happy. Maybe he needed to apply himself more as Soul always told him. One can say though, in some cases, Soul could be on some bird feed crap.

Something was wrong with Soul; he say any and everything out his mouth, and he didn't give a fuck. Plus, half the time, he couldn't get what he was trying to say out, old funny stutter all the time. Look, look, here he goes now, can hear Soul say, "Ro-roo-room an-and board fa-foo-food an-and all." As men, we should understand that we have our own to take care of. Though dawgs were all in this together, because all the partners were chasing the tissue, never steal from the hand that's feeding you.

Man, Chief was telling Loco about how DE showed him the brick of dough (money) and slid some out the middle. Talking about "these niggas don't want to pay me," so you know Loco put Zee up on game.

"Real life! Yo living off the land, then he does whatever he wants with the packs and so on," Zee said.

CHAPTER 15

Prodigal Son

NEVER MIND ALL that; this was just an introduction of the hour, and Boss Hog moment was up. Boss Hog! Let me tell you—a big biker white man who lived in the block for as long as one could remember. One thing about Boss Hog, he brought a lot of money to the Hill. All night long, rocking off in Hog's grandfolk's house, his grandparents own two houses in the block. Hog's mother and his two sons live in the other house across the street. Now guess Yo was trying to make a statement or something. Bro knew that wasn't good for the team; he wanted his voice to be heard. Didn't know that he was just going about it the wrong way. Man! Bro just started rocking shit! Before you know it, homeys running around the shack talking about somebody stretch Boss Hog's ass out. Comrades saw several bodies in the streets before, but this was vivid. Hog's body was laid out on the side of Brenda's house. He was on the sidewalk facedown as soon as you turn in the block. Chief and Loco walked up Jefferson to see what the deal was. Man! They kept it pushing; Loco was kind of mad because shit was about to be hot. Plus, it's a Caucasian dude in the hood. Then on top of it, Boss Hog was a major contributor to the block. Comrades running around laughing at the ordeal. Zee didn't find a damn thing funny; he was just wondering how Comrades let this go down. Boss Hog was just lying there, but the ill thing was how long. He was dead on the curb for about twenty-five minutes. Nobody even called the police, ambulance, or anything until Nardo knocked on Boss Hog's door and told Hog's son.

"Yo, your father's up on the corner stretched out," Nardo said.

The heat was about to come down on the block. Individuals knew the dough flow was going to be slow.

"Fuck was all that about, luv?" Chief asked.

"He owes me some dough!" Nigga said.

"Money! How much?" Chief asked.

"It wasn't the dough. It was the point, principle, whatever. Y'all all know how that racist whore be," Nigga said.

"Man, whatever! How much?" Chief asked.

"Fifty dollars," Nigga said.

"Shit, Nigga, I wouldn't have giving you that," Loco said.

"No, you wouldn't; if I had said something to you about it. You would have said, "Fuck 'em shot 'em," Nigga said.

"Yeah, you're probably right, but what the hell, he was worth more alive than dead," Loco said.

"Fuck it! He's gone now, and shit 'bout to be on round this bitch. I'm 'bout to get the fuck away from here," Chief said.

Poor white trash authorities didn't give a fuck about Boss Hog—an old biker, drug addict with a record as long as your arm. Things were right back to normal on the Hill. It was like Hog was a nigga in the ghetto. Until Hog's funeral, one is not gonna hold you (lie to you). Dawgs were shook; it was every bit off a hundred bikers in the block, all dirty-looking white men with long hair. The Hill just knew they were on some payback terms. Dawgs all got outa there, let that man RIP. Fuck all that thug life shit; dudes wouldn't go fucking with them. Hell's angels ass niggas now that was something to laugh about; the hill didn't want any trouble (no smoke). It was Boss Hog Hill that day, and dawgs didn't have any problem with it.

Capone dumb ass a brick, packing (joking) on the way down the hill, talking about, "Shit, man, this used to be an all-white community anyway," El-Capone said.

CHAPTER 16

Not a Game

All mob up down Stephanie smoking and bullshitting. Stephanie's house was on Milton and Jefferson at the top of the Hill. Nardo's sister left the house to him and Stephanie's. Nardo's sister just couldn't stomach the neighborhood anymore after losing her mother in a house fire. The Hill was thugging in that bitch. Anyway, this was the jump-out-the-window house. The house was anything—house parties, running drugs, and anything else you could think of. And like one says, the game's played on the Hill. Look right, as you should know, because it was said before if you fall to sleep around players, your ass is grass. Even if you were in someone's house in the hood, you had to be in your own home where your mom's at; anywhere else on the Hill is fair game. You couldn't be in a shack, some trap, or just a little rat hole you ran up in. Definitely, don't go out on the Hill.

Yes, sir! Comrades were on their best bullshit, always going to sleep on people's steps. Neighbor always had to wake these idiots up, and if it wasn't the neighbors, it was the fiends or the police. And all of them say the same thing: "Y'all need to take y'all asses in the house." Come to think about it dawgs were straight-slipping (unaware of surroundings), nigga's had pills on them, tools (guns), and everything.

The Hill didn't give a fuck, and the neighborhood knew it. So that's how the big hand came into play. If you were sleeping on some steps around the way, smack! Nigga could smack all shit out of you.

Zee wasn't with that left-hand game or snatches, but as the Rabbi said, "It's not a game." Yet the big hand definitely wasn't a game. Get on point, player; dawgs out here thuggin', no time for sleeping. You will get the hell smacked out of you for sleeping before someone come through and blow your brains on the neighbor's door.

Fellas geeking down Stephanie's on that fire shit now. Dawgs put matches in comrades' toes or alcohol on their trousers. It didn't matter; we had no picks. Anybody could get it if you were caught slipping. I mean comrades walking around with burned-up clothes all day long. Yet for some reason, it was always the same people. If it wasn't G-dawg, it was Si, or DE and Raw Man. I am not gonna hold you (lie to you). Raw Man took the cake; he was a straight alcoholic, so niggas straight smacking all shit up out of him in the block. So anyway, G-dawg in the house was knocked out, can't exactly remember who was rolling with the rush, but dawgs was in G-dawg's bushes (lurking, pursuing).

Someone gave Chief some rubbing alcohol; he put it in the front of G's pants where he couldn't feel it. DE was grinning, holding the lighter in his hand. He always had a light, old chain smokin' ass. Chief grabbed that bitch and lit both of G-dawg's legs. Classic, you had to be there to feel or understand this situation. Fuck it! I'll try to explain it to y'all. Poof! Shit ablaze, right? So G-dawg was still out. Now you could hear a pin drop, Cuz hopped straight up out of nowhere. Yelling and cursing, patting the bottom of his legs, all frantic. He was talking about, "Yo, what the fuck, fuck wrong with you, whores!"

The crew started dying laughing, no water or nothing, just let 'em burn. Tears were in Capone's eyes from crying and laughing. G-dawg was still patting his pants down, shaking his head in disgust, mad selling all types of threats, "Watch Ima get ya'll. Watch, I'm get all y'all niggas; It's on!" Now'dudes were talking about calling the fire department, pulling at his clothes all burnt up. Comrades were so fucking ignorant talking 'bout, "That looks like a first-degree burn. Let me see!" One of the homeys dumb ass yelled out.

Like one would say, there never was a dull moment on the Hill. Comrades didn't know what the word *bored* was; it was not in the Hill's vocabulary.

CHAPTER 17

Why?

THIS NIGGA HERE! Around the spot on his drunk shit, that's what he does: get drunk and throw up. Matter of fact, he could just drink a beer and call earl. Mean, this dude just earl (vomiting) for nothing, walking up the street throwing up drinking a 40 oz. Bro had this blue steel .38; well, it was the hood joint. This biscuit (gun) was ugly; the hammer was all loose on it. Comrades hated that gun; this nigga was the only one who like that piece of shit believing he was the only one who knows how to work it. Really don't even want to get into this incident. (Wrote a book about, want to hear it; here it goes.)

Before that dumb shit hit the land, the Hill was straight retarded with it. Bro has a tab and all at the joint. People knew Yo's retarded ass; the owner of the spot knew where Bro was staying at. Come to think of it, these people also owned a house in the block.

"Fuck was, this Nigga thinking of killing the whole place." In the aftermath of the situation, these were the only words that came out of Chief's mouth. Maybe it was too much of that one hundred proof; yeah, old granddaddy that was Yo shit. Guess this nigga waited till they were about to close, still ordering drinks running up the tab. From out of nowhere, this nigga whipped out the blue steel on the bitch and demanded money. Don't know why this silly ass girl bucked (put up fight, resisting) on Bro. Maybe because she knew him and couldn't believe it herself. One couldn't begin to say, I'll explain it this way. Oh yeah, forgot to mention that the woman was a Caucasian lady. Guess her dumb ass thought he was just geeking and brush his arm away with the joint (gun) in his hand. You know what happened next: that piece of shit ass gun went off on her silly ass accidentally hitting her in the stomach somewhere; this nigga straight panic. *Fuck, didn't mea' that* flashed through his mind. She was in a crotch position behind the counter holding her stomach. Nothing else to do now but finish the job.

Bam-bam! Blow her head up, plus, she was kinda bold anyway, thinking she really knew yo like she could talk him out of what he was doing. Now there was another lady working in the joint, and you know what that means. One can remember her now: tall black lady with glasses. That's right; everybody called her Ms. High, can recall both of them being crackheads. Anyway, no witness allowed, so she had to go too.

Pow-pow! With a smile, she fell to the floor believing it was a clean getaway. Bro jumped straight on the register, grabbing the little cash. Forget what year this was, but it was like 95–96. This little hole in the wall (ghetto spot like a bar) was run-down, so the spot had no cameras or anything. Bro did know that about the cameras. What this nigga didn't know was the old lady who owns the joint was in the bathroom in the back. She came out and ran to the back of the place upstairs. Bro licked off a few shots at her old ass. That hundred proof must have gotten to his aim though because he definitely missed her ass. From then on, it's a straight rush. This old lady knew this nigga; he was a loyal customer. Yet that's all she knew though was his nickname. Taking it back in the day on that mob deep shit "temperature rising," even the hood rat chicks were asking questions.

Dawgs didn't know who did what, so stop asking. Yeah, man, they were on it, I mean really in dawgs bushes. So of course, attorneys snatched Zee up. Homicide said people told them Zee and that nigga was riding around the hood in the car together. Zee said, "Man, I don't even know bro like that. He was renting a room from my uncle." Till this day, that nigga didn't believe it, but they snatched his ID out of the house. That's how they found out who he was because they really didn't have anything. Plus, what the fuck could one tell them who wasn't there. Shit! A nigga didn't know nothing. Man, at the time, dawgs didn't even really know each other's government (full name). Yeah, Zee should have gotten rid of the ID like bro asked him to. Yet come on now, you leave that responsibility on the dawg.

People always want to blame others for their fuck ups. Nigga dirty up Zee's name about that dumb ass shit. Up El-Capone's house, Zee said they had a body attachment warrant when they grabbed the ID; that had to count for something. Now the next day, they came back with another warrant and took cloth and shit with blood on them. Plus, one was big cappin' (lying) and for what? They were asking a whole bunch of stupid shit trying to catch a nigga up. One must have slipped off and said something dumb like the last time where he had seen him or something. Yeah, it was Zee's time to go through that shit. This was a learning experience for a nigga. Don't believe Zee could have given his dawg up anyway even though he really didn't know what happened.

"How the fuck you gonna tell somebody something when you not there?" Zee said.

So for all my readers, just stick to the script; you don't know shit. Then that nigga on the line with these crud ball bitches was calling them from another state asking them to go get comrades. Walking up those bitches' house giving them money. Had the girls Western Union him money and they were stealing it too. Top it off, those hoes turned him in. They probably were listening on the phone the whole time. Marshals run straight down on his retard ass all the way up Philly somewhere. Yeah, they give Bro forty-plus for that off-the-wall mess, and they give Yo Boss Hog redrum (murder) too. Comrades say Nardo put them boys on with that.

One day, dawgs were in the block cooling, and Nardo came around, so we were chilling drinking, and something strange was in the air though. They just didn't put Zee up on game because niggas knew Zee had a soft spot for Nardo's bitch ass. Man! Snot smacks all shit up out of Nardo across his forehead with a King Cobra 40 oz. Nardo got the dick look as blood started pouring from his head.

"Why the fuck! Fuck you do that for?" Zee said.

"Man! Y'all know that whore told on Bro," Snot said.

Yeah, back then, niggas ain't play with rats, and the boys were looking for Nardo about that Boss Hog's shit. Nowadays, it's like the plague was out this joint, and everybody has one as a pet in their hood.

CHAPTER 18

Hit Man's Target

Now El-Capone had just come home, and Zee was getting to it on the block, as usual, giving it up. So when Ms. Peaches insisted on copping coke from Capone, one knew something wasn't right. Till this day, Zee knew them niggas up the street had something to do with that hit. Before we get all into this attempt, let's run it back a little for y'all. So we can understand the significance of the target. When Zee first came around the way, one day, Zee and El-Capone were out cooling on Jefferson Street, smoking and drinking. Then all of a sudden, Bro's face went pale like he saw a ghost or something. Hell, damned near scared the shit out of Zee, and he only fears God.

"What's up, bro? Fuck's wrong with you?" Zee asked.

"That's Yo!" El-Capone said.

"Who?" Zee asked.

"Dude Snow. He killed Mack, my road dawg, a couple years ago," El-Capone said.

Zee looked up, and it was a bald big head nigga in a white Land Cruiser with ski racks on the top.

Capone looked straight at Zee with bloodshot red eyes. "Yo, a favor for a favor, if you ever see that nigga and you nappy (carrying gun), get him for me, and I'll owe up one."

Shit! Zee just complied; he just came around the way. Nigga wasn't even no killer like that he was always about the money. And this dude had it. Whoever the fuck he was. This dude Snow had half of East Baltimore on lock, and he was doing his thing over west. Snow was feeding a lot of people. I mean this nigga had stores and all that shit. Shit Zee prayed to God he didn't have to fulfill that obligation. Zee knew that shit would be nothing but trouble. Plus, he wanted some of the bricks everybody was getting. Nine times out of ten, the coke or dope we had was coming from him anyway. See, with El-Capone, it wasn't about the money, and one understood that. When it comes down to a dawgs life, there is no price.

So a few years went by, maybe three, and we came upon these moments, and it was still like the 95–96. Remember now, Comrades were still staying at the house on Orleans street. Recalling El-Capone running down the house to get the hammer, Comrades were on the corner of the block.

"This whore got some nerve he just like fuck us, huh?" El-Capone said.

Give a look down the street to see what this nigga fussing about. And what do you know, it's this big head bald nigga. By this time, one can really care less. Dawgs were out knocking (selling a lot of drugs) on the block. Guess by so many years gone by, this dude was straight sleeping' He never thought he was gone to get any kickback about Mack.

See, El-Capone never let that shit go. By the time a nigga looks up, Capone has a mask and tool in hand, walking down on him. Bro hit Montford to come around the back way. This dude was really slipping (unaware of surroundings) in the next block of Port down by the laundromat. Talking to some bitch that just moved in the last house at the corner by the alley, snake alley at that. Now the bitch was a redbone, a bum too. Guess he saw the potential in her. She was bad if you put a couple dollars on her. Plus, the house was right at the alley.

I didn't know how he didn't see Cuz run down on him. Bro must have hit that split in the alley and you right at the back door. Then Bro popped out on Snow! Now Comrades were right there on Port looking down at the whole ordeal. Bro got to knocking. "Knock-knock!" Snow pushed the bitch in front of him. She was in the door, and snow had one leg up on the steps too busy mackin' (trying to get with shorty). Capone threw her ass out the way; she ran down the street yelling. That shit looked kind of wired the way she was waving her hands and all. Snow tried to run in the house, and my nigga followed suit.

From there on, all you heard was knocking. Capone was in that bitch nailing Snow to the floor. Bro came out of the house and walked halfway up the block, pulled the mask off, and walked toward us. Eyes of fury, these were the eyes of a pure killer. Capone hit the alley where them niggas had shot Face from. And why the fuck he dropped the biscuit (gun) in a bucket of water right in that alley? Don't ask how one know all this, but niggas do dumb shit in the heat of the moment.

There's been a dark cloud over the Hill 'till this day. The Port Street niggas ain't shit; that was all you heard. For this reason, El-Capone became a hit man's target. There has been money on El-Capone's head for as long as one could remember. You wouldn't believe how many attempts on El-Capone's life there were. That's what brings us to this attempt. Ms. Peaches was talking about how she wants Capone stuff. In Zee's mind, he's like, *Hold up; I am the coke king of the block.* Before you know it, a navy-blue Chevy Cavalier rode down the block and called out, "Ellsworth, Ellsworth." His dumbass was so caught up about the sale thinking it was some more action.

The whole time, pop, pop, pop, hitting El-Capone all in his chest! Zee ran to the bando to grab the tone (gun), but when Zee came back out of the house, the car was outa there. El-Capone came up out of that hit. Just one of many attempts on El-Capone's life. This was like a month or two after the Snow episode that just happened. Capone damn near buried the joint in the bando because it was the one used on Snow.

El-Capone has been hit so many times you could write a book about it. Everybody took a shot at Bro, but some things weren't meant to be. El-Capone's cause must have been justified by his action. Nobody could drop him; even the police used to call Cuz nine lives, bulletproof, etc. And for this, Bro was truly psycho with a schizophrenic paranoid demeanor. El-Capone didn't trust anybody. Not even his day ones, his own dawgs. Could you blame him? El-Capone was definitely ahead of his time. Capone used to do a bunch of off-the-wall shit, but nowadays, Comrades understand it.

The Hill could go on and on about El-Capone. You really can't take nothing from him though. El-Capone really made the Hill what it was. Comrades were really running behind dawg like, "Thug life! What bitch! Death before dishonor!"

CHAPTER 19

Three Js

BACK TO THE block and the plot of things. Mino! Shit ball of a nigga, one means he just ain't shit no do right to save his life. Don't even know why a nigga was writing about his stupid ass. Beside the fact that he was El-Capone, Chief, and Si's cousin, Zee never wanted shit to do with him. Now he comes into play in this scenario, for some can be the demise of others. Zee just came home from his first bit (doing time in jail). He came from boot camp, so it was like around 96–97, but he was cooling.

See, one remembered Chief kept trying to get Zee to put him on with the plug. Chief was like, "Come on, son, I'm telling you it's out here! Hold up, bro; look at this donkey here. He's straight-launching! Yo got the candy apple red Land Cruiser little gold watch and shit." Chief had sized Candy Apple Yo up real quick, looking real good. Shit was stiff (nothing happened) around the way, and Chief was on his spot rushing (robbing) shit. A little bit too much of that purple tape in his mind. Because to Chief, this nigga definitely look like a happy meal. Chief was like, "Oh yeah, youngin gone holla at May on Jefferson, he just don't know where he at."

Before you could say a word, Bro came around the corner bandit and all. Straight smack all shit out this dude with the ratchet (gun) off the jump. Let him know it was real on this Hill. Chief threw Apple Red Yo in his cruiser then got to running through his pockets, hit the glove box, straight-jacking.

Chief said, "Okay, got your dumb ass, you holding two I should kill your bitch ass. Bet not never see you round this way again, or I am flat line your ass."

Man! Zee got the fuck outa there, didn't want Apple to see his face and put him in all that shit. Zee was on his bootcamp shit; he wasn't with none of that dumb shit. Now Mino was the father of the retardo bots. Chief was a hustler, so one really can't begin to tell you how these two fools got hooked up together besides the fact that they are cousins. So as it was said that Mino got to dealing with this dude named J from up the hill somewhere. Now what made things interesting was Mino took Chief up there one day with him and introduced Chief to J. So this was how they became familiar with Chief. Then this fool Mino took J off for some pills or something. Mino came around the back, climbed through the window, and took their shit after they left the house. Yet them niggas must have been on to him.

J was looking for this fool Mino; they rolled through the way looking for Mino on the regular. And guess who happened to pop up, yep, your boy Chief. Now I don't know if Chief had any idea of what his cousin had done. But he knows that Mino is a dickhead. So why the fuck would Chief go to the car when the whores called him. When he knew they were looking for Mino's simple ass, Chief was leaning over in the car talking to the dude J. Don't know actually what they were saying, but Chief's face started to look distressed. Then out of the blue, bang-bang-bang! Right out the car. Chief broke down the block running full blast holding his chest. Bro collapsed midway right before you hit the alley. Everything was moving so fast, but for him to catch his breath, it was taking so long. Chief started breathing so slowly, eyes to the sky talking to him but he gave no reply. At the time, nobody even knew who was in the car but Chief and G-dawg. And G-dawg didn't put comrades on that until afterward; we wouldn't have known what happened or where this shit came from. That was just how things popped off on the Hill; you never know who is gonna bend the corner.

El-Capone used to always say, "What's gonna happen, gonna happen." Zee of all people understands when it's your time, it's you time. Now you live and learn, and what one has learned is we create our own condition. So *living* is the keyword here. Live!

Zee's baby's mother came into the house hysterically. He didn't know if she was hurt or happy. She was like, "Oh my gosh, I just saw your homeboy Ells with blood all over him and tiremarks on his shirt." So I looked at him and like, "What the fuck?" He said, "Jerimiah tried to run me over with the car." In Gem's mind, *He did try to kill you ass.* Shit didn't surprise Zee at all; fools always try to take Capone out. But she was dying laughing. She didn't know what to think, just shaking her head. So Zee slid up the way to see what the fuck was going on. Dawgs were beefing with the fools right up the street from them. Now this shit was ill too; if Zee was on the Hill, this shit would have never transpired for the simple fact that Zee was born and raised up the street. On Duncan and Jefferson, Zee hit his first pack (a number of pills). Plus, he knows everybody up the street, and he has people up that way; shit, it's only three blocks away. Zee was like the mediator because he was brought up with these Duncan Street dudes. Ellswroth (a.k.a. El-Capone) didn't like any of them and envied Zee for coming from up that way.

So when Zee came through on the Hill, El-Capone didn't have a shirt on wiping blood off him. All he was talking about was killing that whore.

"Your bitch boy tried to kill me with the car," El-Capone said.

"Who you talking 'bout. I ain't never fuck wit that nigga; what happened?" Zee said.

"Asshole Jeremiah ran me over with the car. I'm kill that bitch when I catch him. Fucks up with you Sergeant Zee, fuck brings you around?" El-Capone said.

This nigga was being sarcastic; they know Zee was on his chill shit just coming home from bootcamp, and this was how he became the name General.

"For real! I came up here to make sure you were all right," Zee said.

"Yeah, I did see Gem" El-Capone said.

That was just how Capone was; he wanted to see Zee's attention. He knew Zee already knew what happened; he just wanted to see where Zee was at with it. Zee was like the mediator between the hoods, and by him not hanging around, the way shit became kind of fucked up with them dudes up the street. After Chief's funeral, day by day, slowly, Zee began to creep back and forth through the hood.

Before you know it, Zee is back around the way up to the same old tricks, but now he's the General, and it's straight thugging.

CHAPTER 20

Loco

Now Loco was on the run for a body. Matter of fact, I think he beat that body. One doesn't remember what the fuck Loco was on the run for. Yet one has to learn a valuable lesson in running from your fate. Sometimes, you just have to sit down and get your mind in the right place. Prison saves many men even though one wishes prison upon no one. Here to tell you to deal with the situation as men do. Trust and believe you will come through the fire refined like gold roaming to and fro somewhere on the hill. Nevertheless, Zee wasn't around when this old head dude came through the block. Now understand the scenario of things. How a little fire can spread. Old dude came through patting the bottom of his cigarette pack walking up the block.

So Capone said, "Let me get a cigarette, uncle."

Now Uncle got slick with El-Capone on some old school slang.

"Fuck you! You lucky, I don't knock your old ass out and take the whole pack bitch!" El-Capone said.

Anyway, to make a long story short, Uncle got out of there. Take note that this was early in the day. So now it's nighttime around eight or ten, something like that. Comrades were out here chilling. Forget what the hell dawgs were into at the time, but know that Zee was chasing that tissue (money). El-Capone and a few other dawgs grouped up with this one dude Zee knew from playing basketball with.

Let's slide away from the scene for one minute to express the dealing of Zee's cruddy buddies. Real quick, let's go back to the future because, the whole time, these cruddy motherfuckers were huddled up over there. They were planning on selling the chopper. The fucked-up part was that the XM-15 (semi-automatic gun) was missing a month ago. Zee and Mark-5 went half on it anyway. So Zee wasn't so worried about it even though Zee's arm was stronger than Mark-5. They could have still put Zee up in the game. Maybe the situation wouldn't have gone down the way it did, just for wishful thinking. After all, what's done is done.

Rye-Dawg came up the way and went to hide his biscuit in the back alley yard. Now this was two weeks after the whole Uncle thing. When he stumbled upon the XM-15 back under the porch, the whole time they were trading the chopper for two handguns. Wow! Your own being cruddy stealing the XM-15 from ourselves. It was in the bando for a case such as this. Guess cruddy buddies didn't want Zee to know what they were doing. Plus, come to think about it: that night, buddies were out back in the alley testing it out. Now recalling that night, that night, Loco had just come around the way. He all spoke out and shit on the run.

Zee said, "Fuck up with your scary ass?"

Loco said, "Shit, just came out of the house. I am out this bitch!"

Capone and them were still huddled up by Yo's truck which Zee used to hoop with. Guess he was the one trading the hand joints. All of a sudden, out of nowhere, Uncle popped up out of the blue, pointing his finger at El-Capone talking about that's the one with two of his nephews by his side. Comrades were talking about something, not paying dude and his nephew no mind. Now in Zee's mind, he is like, *These fools are either holding (carrying guns) crazy or just don't know where the fuck they are.* Zee never saw these dudes a day in his life and couldn't tell you who they were if he saw them again.

Back to wishful thinking, Zee would have gone and grabbed that XM-15 if he had known where it was at that moment. So Uncle was pointing and yelling his shit with his nephew on deck. Now if anybody knew Capone, you are in the wrong block with all that dumb shit. First, El-Capone was about to jump straight out the window until the nigga who was trading the joints with Capone grabbed him and like fuck all that. To Zee's surprise, El didn't feed into that shit the old man was talking about; they all just frivolously waved their hands at Uncle. "Go ahead with that bullshit." Here, Zee goes to save the day.

Zee said, "Uncle, now you know how niggas are these days. You are too old for all this bullshit; as long as a motherfucker ain't put his hands on you, there shouldn't be any problem. Then you bring your people around here and shit. Come on now! I know you better than that."

The whole time, Zee walked away from the crowd heading out the block talking to Uncle with his two nephews on his heels. They ain't saying nothing the whole time. Zee remembered talking to the one dude face-to-face because a dawg knew he was nappy (carrying a gun). The other dude was short ruddy built; he just followed suit. Lo and behold out the mother fuckin' blue, Zee almost had them niggas out the block. Niggas were by the killer hill wall the first house on Jefferson, the backyard corner house on Port. This Capone nigga, he started calling Uncle.

"Uncle, Uncle, fuck you was talking 'bout now," El-Capone said.

It's Capone, Hooping Yo, and Loco following behind El.

The old man said in a bold voice, "Yeah, you said you were gonna hit me in the mouth."

Why did Uncle say that? Before you could bat an eye, El-Capone stole (sneak hit) all shit out the old dude. Then everything was like slow motion; it seemed like it took Uncle forever to hit the ground. This shit really baffled Zee because the next word that came out Capone's mouth was detrimental.

Uncle finally hit the ground inside the gateway of the wall yard. You would not believe what this nigga said next. I'm not gonna hold you (lie to); it was some gangster shit, but this ain't no movie Ellsworth. Zee was ready to grab one of them niggas, and the question was, "Why Capone didn't knock one of the nephews out? They were the threat?" Plus, he knew this because guess what he said? "Pull out your gun now, bitch!" And that was what the fuck nephew did.

Bang. Bang. Bang! It hit El-Capone dead on three straight to the gut. Then he threw one at Hooping Yo. How Nephew caught Loco on the run with a slug to the back, no one even knew. Zee was sure glad he didn't try to grab Nephew; he'll probably be dead right now.

(Pull out your gun now, bitch!) Nigga got to cutting loose on his physico ass. Zee just ran over to Brenda's; really, he just ran straight across from where they were. If Nephew wanted to, that fool could have hit Zee too. Remember, he was just in their face talking to them. Guess he didn't feel like Zee was a threat. Slide back through the little split from Loco's old yard to Brenda's yard. You have El-Capone laid in the middle of the block. He's on his regular routine, laying there calm, not panicking or nothing. He was just still like he was dead. Hooping Yo was crying like a son of a bitch. "Call the ambulance," while holding his stomach.

Zee took a glance to the corner; he heard a car peeling off. He saw the old man trying to make it around the corner. So Zee was now at the corner to see if he could take a glimpse of the car that the nephews were in. Next thing you know, the whole Hill was jumping on Uncle Yo. Hell yeah! These idiots left the old man behind. Man, they got to jumping off steps on the old man's head while others were kicking him in the face. One even saw a comrade slam a cinder block on his head.

Zee shook his head figuring that Yo Uncle must be dead. Zee banged back down the block to see another dawg laying in the alley. In Zee's mind, he was like, *Yo only shoot four or five times and hit three people, fuck*!" Zee didn't even know Loco was hit too. Shit, he knew Nephew caught El-Capone with three straight. "Damn!" Zee hollered as he ran over to Loco lying in the alley right by his old house. He was calling Zee.

"Zee, Zee, Zee, help me, Yo! I can't feel my legs!" Loco said in a low, calm tone.

Zee kneeled down to him and said, "Like where you hit, Cuz?"

All Loco kept saying was he can't feel his legs. Then he started to go out on a nigga.

"Loco, Loco!" Zee was yelling his name. Laid out with him in the alley, smacking his face in disbelief. "What the fuck you doing,

Cuz! Don't panic on me, bro, you good man; stop panicking dawg! Yo! You been shot before Cuz. Come on, man, this ain't shit. Breathe, my nigga, breath. It's all right. You gonna be all right. Loc, Loc, Loco!"

ABOUT THE AUTHOR

SUNNI RINGGOLD LIVED a life of ignorance and incarceration until he utilized his experiences and gravitated to opportunities around him and dedicated himself to writing and walking a higher path of enlightenment. Sunni Ringgold was born and raised in Baltimore City, just a few blocks away from the world-renowned John Hopkins Hospital. Sunni lost his father at the age of nine and is fortunate among a host of associates, family, and peers to survive in the trenches of Baltimore City.

CPSIA information can be obtained
at www.ICGtesting.com
Printed in the USA
BVHW040214210523
664488BV00002B/441

9 781684 984442